JEANNETTE CAINES

WINDOW WISHING

Illustrated by Kevin Brooks

Harper & Row, Publishers

Window Wishing

 Printed in the United States of America. For information address Harper & Row, Publishers, Inc., 10 East 53rd Street, New York, N.Y. 10022. Published simultaneously in Canada by Fitzhenry & Whiteside Limited, Toronto.
First Edition

Library of Congress Cataloging in Publication Data
Caines, Jeannette Franklin.
Window wishing.

SUMMARY: A sister and brother spend a vacation with their fun and unconventional grandmother.

[1. Grandmothers–Fiction] I. Brooks, Kevin.
II. Title.
PZ7.C12Wi 1980 [E] 79-2698
ISBN 0-06-020933-X
ISBN 0-06-020934-8 (lib. bdg.)

For:

Momatillie & Grandma Mag

Deux grand-mères formidables

Bootsie and I spend our vacations
with Grandma Mag.
She wears sneakers all the time.

Sometimes we walk barefooted
on the cement.
Grandma says it makes your toes strong.

She makes the best lemonade
with just one lemon,
and we drink it out of our own mugs.
Bootsie's is green and mine is purple.

Grandma raises worms and she fishes,
and she can make a kite.

She lets Bootsie and me set the table
with different-colored dishes
and mix-matched forks
that she's saved for 200 years.

Grandma doesn't like to cook.
But we always have gingersnaps and cheese
with sassafras tea for dessert.

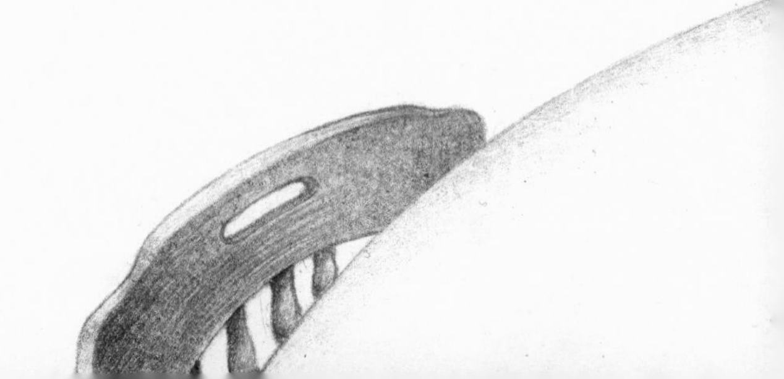

YUMMY
BRAND
GINGER
SNAPS

PICKLES

After dinner we get our bikes
and ride downtown and window wish.
Grandma says when she was little
she would catalog wish.

Mondays and Wednesdays
are my wish days.

Tuesdays and Thursdays
are Bootsie's.

Saturday is Grandma's wish day.
Every Saturday
we have a picnic at the cemetery
where Grandpa Ben is buried.

I always get nervous, but Grandma says
it's the most peaceful place to have a picnic.

She doesn't let us wish on Sundays.
After church
Grandma likes to read the Sunday comics.
She says she and Orphan Annie
are the same age.

THE DAILY

Next week is a special week.
Bootsie gets to wish every day –
it's his birthday.

W9-DDH-046

Taking Your Camera to CHINA

Ted Park

Raintree Steck-Vaughn Publishers
A Harcourt Company

Austin · New York
www.steck-vaughn.com

Published by Raintree Steck-Vaughn Publishers,
an imprint of Steck-Vaughn Company

Library of Congress Cataloging-in-Publication Data available upon request.

Printed in the United States of America
10 9 8 7 6 5 4 3 2 1 W 03 02 01 00

Cover photo: The Great Wall of China

Photo acknowledgments

Contents

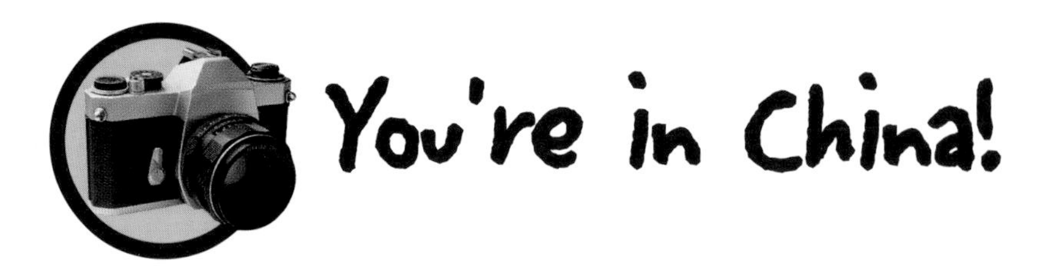

You're in China!

China is located in eastern Asia. It is a nation of tall mountains, deserts, and **farmland**. The Chinese call their country Zhongguo, which means *Middle Country*. The name comes from the ancient Chinese who thought their country was the center of the world. Ancient means something that is very old. China is an ancient country whose **culture** is thousands of years old. Culture is the way of life, beliefs, and traditions of a group of people.

There are several interesting cities in China. The largest city in China is **Shanghai**. It has a population of more than 14 million people. The name Shanghai means *upon the water.*

China is the third largest country in the world. More than 1.2 billion people live there today. This means that one in every five people in the world lives in China. More people live in China today than in any other country.

Behind these farmers are rice terraces. Farmers dig into a mountain to build them. Some are thousands of years old.

This book will show you some of the best things to see in China. You will learn interesting things about the country and the people who live there. So, when you're ready to take your camera there, you'll know exactly what to do and where to go. Enjoy your trip!

Looking at the Land

China is roughly 3,100 miles (4988 km) from east to west and 3,400 miles (5471 km) from north to south. It has an area of 3,696,000 square miles (9,572,640 sq km), which makes it a little larger than the United States. Russia and Canada are the only two countries that are larger than China. The city of Shanghai, one of China's most important seaports, is located on China's eastern coast.

Mountains and Deserts

Two thirds of the country is either mountain or desert. **Mt. Everest**, the world's tallest mountain, is on the border of China and Nepal. Mt. Everest is 29,028 feet (8,845 m) high.

There are different kinds of deserts. The **Gobi Desert** is in the north of China and to the south of Mongolia. It is the second largest desert in the world. The Gobi Desert measures about 500,000 square miles

Irtysh
Irtysh
Ulaanbaatar
MONGOLIA
GOBI DESERT
Turpan
Tarim R.
TAKLIMAKAN DESERT
CHINA
Beijing
Tianjin
Huang He River
Huang He River
Huang He River
Huang He River
NORTH KOREA
Pyongyang
Seoul
SOUTH KOREA
Sea of Japan
Yellow Sea
JAPAN
Indus
Chiang Jiang River (Yangtze)
Chang Jiang R.
Shanghai
East China Sea
N
W
E
S
Pacific Ocean
INDIA
NEPAL
Kathmandu
Mount Everest
Ganges
Ganges
Brahmaputra
Salween R.
Mekong
Mekong
Formosa Str.
Hong Kong
Gulf of Tonkin
South China Sea
CHINA
International Boundary
National Capital
Major Cities
Rivers
Mountain
0
500 Miles
0
500 KM

Sir Edmund Hilary and his Sherpa guide Tenzing Norgay were the first people to reach the top of Mt. Everest in 1953.

(1,294,900 sq km). It is referred to as a rock and shifting desert. The **Taklimakan Desert** is another large desert. In fact, it measures about 105,000 square miles (272,000 square km). It is one of the largest sandy deserts in the world. Imagine all that sand!

Great Rivers of China

China has two large rivers: the **Chang**, which is also known as the Yangtze River, and the **Huang He**, also

known as the Yellow River. The Yangtze is the longest river on the Continent of Asia, and the third longest in the world. A continent is one of the large landmasses that make up the world. Each of these rivers waters hundreds of thousands of square miles of farmland. This makes the land usable for farming. The rivers make the eastern half of China one of the best-watered farm areas in the world.

Does this look like a desert? In a rock and shifting sand desert like the Gobi, the wind blows the sand from place to place. That's the reason why you can't see big sand dunes in this picture.

Beijing

China's Capital

Beijing is the capital city of China. It is China's second largest city and has more than eleven million people. For many years, the city was called *Peking*. Peking means northern capital.

Beijing is a beautiful city that is famous for its parks, lakes, and **temples**. A temple is a building used for worshiping, like a church. The Beijing Zoo is also known throughout the world for its pandas.

Beijing is the center for business too. It is the political and financial center of China. It is also an important location for the manufacturing, communications, and transportation industries.

An Ancient City

The inner city dates back to the 8th century B.C. It is called the **Forbidden City**. It was built more than 500

Over time, 24 emperors have lived in the Forbidden City. It is now the Imperial Palace museum.

years ago as the palace for the **emperor**. Over 200,000 workers built it. It was named the Forbidden City because most people were forbidden to enter. Only the emperor could go into some parts of the city. Now the Forbidden City is mainly museums. If you go there, maybe you can take a snapshot of one of China's most beautiful art treasures. Don't forget to take your camera!

Tiananmen Square is located here, too. It is the site of large celebrations. It is also where Chinese students protested against the government to gain more freedom in 1989.

Great Places to Visit

The first place you'll want to stop is **The Great Wall**. It is the only man-made object that can be seen from space. It begins in the mountains of Korea and runs to the Gobi Desert.

The Great Wall was built and rebuilt over 1000 years. Some parts were built as early as 300 B.C., while newer parts date from A.D. 1368 to 1642. The Great Wall was built to stop attacks by nomads from Mongolia, a country to the north of China.

The Great Wall of China is 4,500 miles (7,300 km) long and 30 feet (9.1 m) tall. Most of it is made of earth, stone, and brick.

Can you believe that at Ch'in Tomb there are more than 7,500 clay men that were made over 2,000 years ago?

Clay Men

Make sure you stop by to see the terra cotta or clay warriors in the Ch'in Tomb. The Ch'in Tomb is located near the city of Xian. This group of clay men is a part of the burial place of the first emperor of China, **Shih huang-ti**.

The People

Dynasties

China's history is divided into periods of time called **dynasties**. Dynasties are time periods that have the name of the families who ruled at that time. The first dynasty was the Qin. The Qin dynasty was the first to bring the Chinese people together into one nation. The Qin dynasty began building the Great Wall in 214 B.C.

Languages and cultures

Most of the people who live in China are natives. Natives are the Han Chinese people who make up 94 percent of the population. Mongol, Korean, and Manchu Chinese, make up most of the rest of the population.

Mandarin Chinese is the official language but people in different parts of China speak different forms of the Chinese language. There are at least eight other forms of Chinese languages spoken.

These people are making noodles. The Chinese people introduced the world to making noodles. Did you know that Marco Polo brought pasta to Europe after he traveled to China?

How Do People Live in China?

Family is important in Chinese culture. Often many generations of a family live together in the same home.

Most families live in the countryside. Most houses have three or four rooms. The older homes are made of mud bricks and have a straw roof. Newer homes are made of

Much of the farm work in China is done by hand. Here, two women sort peppers outside their home.

Here's a great view of Nanpu Bridge in Shanghai. Shanghai is one of China's most overcrowded cities.

clay bricks or stone and have a tile roof. Some villages have built apartment buildings. Most houses have electricity.

Families who live in the city are assigned an apartment by the factory where they work. Most apartments have plumbing and heating and are small. China's cities are overcrowded. A place to live can be hard to find. Sometimes, two families need to share an apartment.

Government and Religion

Government

China's official name is the People's Republic of China. In a Republic people have the power to elect others to manage the government. Elect means to choose someone by voting. It is made up of 22 provinces, which are like states. Three cities that are treated like provinces because of their size are:

- Beijing
- Shanghai
- Tianjin

China has been a communist country for more than 50 years. Communism means people work for the government and are taken care of by the state. There is a president and a premier. Elections are held, but they are controlled by a single party. The government has controlled the people in China for a long time. Now China receives more information and trades with the outside world.

This is a Buddhist ceremony at the Gold Hill Temple. People come here to honor family members who lived long ago.

Religion

Confucianism, **Taoism**, and **Buddhism** are the major religions throughout most of China. Confucianism is based on the ideas of Confucius, a Chinese philosopher who was born about 550 B.C. Taoism is also a native Chinese religion. It teaches that a person should live in harmony with nature. The religious beliefs of many of the Chinese people include elements of all three religions, but the main religion in China is Buddhism. In this religion, people believe that knowledge is very important.

Earning a Living

Almost three fourths of Chinese people are farmers, but only about 10 percent of the land can be farmed. In some areas, farmers are able to harvest crops two or three times a year. Harvest means to pick or gather plants for food. Farming is still done by hand. Major crops include grains, rice, cotton, and tea. China's great rivers, the Yangtze and the Yellow Rivers, help to water these crops. They also raise cattle, pigs, and sheep, and export fish. Export means to send things outside of the country and sell them for a profit.

Other ways to earn a living are textile manufacturing and oil production. The woman on the next page works in the textile industry. Minerals found in China include tungsten, coal, iron, lead, and tin.

China's population is the world's largest workforce. Markets in the United States and around the world are filled with products made in China.

Look at this woman ▶ making a silk cloth. This is an industry the Chinese introduced to the world.

▼ This is a mill where iron and steel is made. It is another way Chinese people earn a living.

School and Sports

Almost three fourths of Chinese people can read and write. Children start school when they are seven years old and must attend school for nine years. They go to school six days a week. Classes are often large and crowded and the school day is long.

Scholars have always been important in Chinese culture, but there are not enough universities for everyone.

Did you know that ping pong is one of the most popular sports in China? Here, some school children from Beijing take a break to play a game.

There is no Chinese alphabet. The characters you see in this picture can sometimes stand for words. The characters sound different depending on what form of Chinese the person speaks.

Soccer and badminton are popular sports in China. The martial arts have been a tradition in China for a long time. Exercise is a part of daily life, especially before going to school or work.

Food and Holiday Fun

Let's Eat!

Cooked rice or noodles are usually eaten with every meal. People add sauces, stir-fried vegetables, fish, and sometimes meat. They also use vegetables such as bean sprouts, bamboo shoots, and water chestnuts. In China, chicken and pork are more popular than beef. All the ingredients are stirred together in a pan known as a wok. A wok is a deep, bowl shaped pan for frying food. The most popular drink is tea.

Celebrate!

During the Chinese New Year, there are many parades and dancing in the streets. Children are given small gifts of coins wrapped in red paper.

Other holidays include May Day and International Workers' Day. They celebrate People's Republic on October 1st.

The Chinese New Year is celebrated in early February. If you go there, get a snapshot of this dragon dance.

The Future

If you took your camera to China, you would see the ancient and the new right next to each other. You would also see a country that is changing.

After 50 years under communism, China has made enormous strides. Even though China is a communist country, some people own their own businesses.

Reducing the population is a key goal for the future. Billboards around the country promote the one-child only campaign. The government rewards families that have just one child. The government believes reducing the population is one way for China to become a modern country.

The Three Gorges Dam will be the largest dam in the world once it's finished. The dam is being built on the Yangtze River west of Yichang. It was started in 1994 and will not be complete until 2014. The dam will control the flooding of the Yangtze River and will generate electricity.

The Chinese are eager to become a modern country. They want to have a better place to live. When you leave

The Victoria Harbor in Hong Kong shows just how beautiful a modern city can be.

China, someone may say to you Zai jian (zigh jee-in). In English, it means, good-bye.

Quick Facts About CHINA

Capital
Beijing

Borders
Mongolia, Russia, Korea, Pakistan, Afghanistan, Tajikistan, Kyrgyzstan, Kazakstan, Vietnam, Laos, Myanmar (Burma), India, Bhutan, and Nepal

Area
3,3696,000 square miles (9,572,640 sq. km)

Population
1,246,871,951

Largest Cities
Shanghai (14,148,000 people)
Beijing (11,299,000 people)

Chief crops
grain, rice, cotton, tea

Natural resources
tungsten, coal, iron, lead, tin, crude oil reserves

Longest river
The Chang Jiang (Yangtze River)–3,915 miles (6,300 km) (third longest in the world)

Flag of China

Coastline
8,700 miles (14,000)

Monetary unit
renminbi (Yuan)

Literacy rate
82 percent of Chinese can read and write

Major industries
iron and steel, textiles and apparel, machine building, armaments, and cement

Glossary

Beijing (BA-jin): The capital city of China. It is also known as Peking.

Buddhism (boo-diz-uhm): A religion from India that places great value in knowledge.

Chang (CHON): This is also known as the Yangtze River. It is the longest river in China and the third largest in the world.

communism (KOM-yuh-niz-um): A concept of government where the people work for and are taken care of by the state.

culture (KUHL-chur): The way of life, beliefs, customs, holidays, and traditions of a group of people.

dynasty (DYE-nuh-stee): A period of time in a China's history when one family or group ruled the nation.

emperor (EM-pur-ur): A ruler or king of a country.

Mt. Everest (mount EV-rast): The tallest mountain in the world; located in Nepal and the province of Tibet in China.

farmland (farm-land): Land used to raise food crops.

Forbidden City (fur-BID-en SIT-ee): The former home of the Emperor and his family in Beijing.

Gobi Desert (GO-bee di-ZURT): A rock and sand desert in northern China and southern Mongolia.

The Great Wall (THUH grayt wawl): A system of stone walls built over 1000 years to protect China from their enemies.

Huang He (hwan hee): This is also known as the Yellow River. It is the second longest river in China.

Mandarin (MAN-dur-in): One of eight dialects of the Chinese language.

Shanghai (SHAN-hi): The largest city in China and one of the largest port cities in the world.

shrines: A special place set aside to honor those who have died.

Taklimakan desert (ta-kle-me-KAN di-ZURT): A sand desert located in northwestern China.

temple: (TEM-puhl) A building where people go to worship.

Index